This Dino Valley Christmas tale is full of dinosaurs.

There's Sid,

Jo,

Jay,

a choir...

two elves,

and even
Santa Claus!

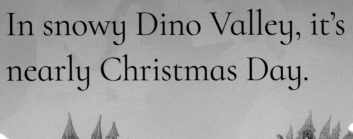

In snowy Dino Valley, it's nearly Christmas Day.

Sid's niece and nephew,
Jo and Jay, have come
to Sid's to stay.

"We're off to visit
Santa Claus.

He's down at Bella's Store."

Wrapped in woollen hats
and scarves...

they head out in the snow.

8

"I've brought my Christmas list," says Jay.

"I've got mine too," adds Jo.

9

They reach the store and meet an elf.

Each shelf they pass
is piled with toys.

"Wow! Look at these,"
says Jay.

"I want this scooter!"
Jo exclaims.

"This robot's cool,"
Jay cries.

"Let's wait and see,"
Sid sighs.

"I've *got* to have this train!" shouts Jay.

He grabs it off the rails.

"I *really* like this bike," yells Jo.

"Please put them back," Sid wails.

Sid takes them up to
Santa's cave.

"Let's go right in," says Jo.

At last the pair
can go inside.

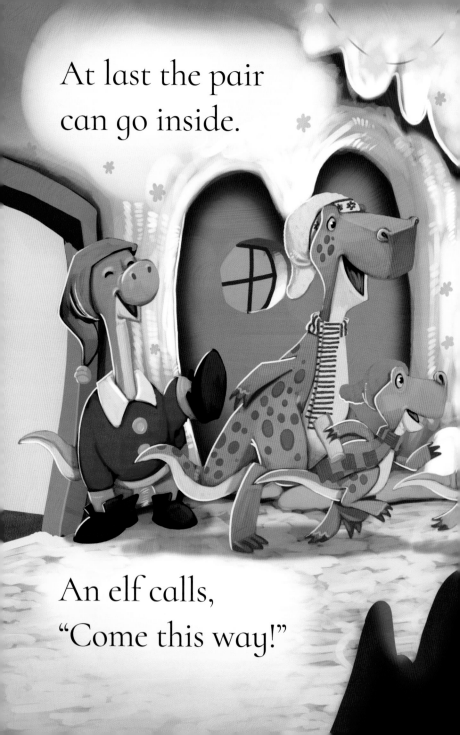

An elf calls,
"Come this way!"

"I know the things I'd like," says Jay.

"I'll tell you what they are...

I want
a watch,

the latest
phone,

a great big
racing car..."

21

"Well..." says Santa.

"Please," says Jay.
"I haven't finished yet...

A tree
house,

skates,

computer
games,

a mini private jet..."

"Don't forget *me*,"
Jo declares. "I'll read my
list out too...

A water slide,

a playground ride,

a pony –
make that two!"

"Well..." says Santa.

"Wait!" says Jo. "I want *more* stuff that's cool.

A sailing boat,

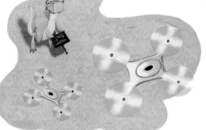

two drones,

a throne,

a full-size
swimming pool..."

27

Then Santa hands them each a gift.

They mumble, "Thank you," looking sad, and slowly stomp away.

Sid's shocked by what
they did.

"What, no toys *at all*?" gasps Jo.

"That's just not fair," cries Jay.

They whisper to each
other, then…

"We have a plan!"
they say.

They hurry back to
Uncle Sid's.

Then, with their pens
and clay...

They make
some cards...

and Christmas stars.

"They're looking great,"
says Jay.

Both Jo and Jay have made new lists.

Soon Jo and Jay
are fast asleep.

Then sleigh bells
ring outside.

The bells wake Jo.

"It's Santa Claus!" Jay cries.

Santa gives them both a wink, then hops back on his sleigh.

"Hey, look! A note!"
says Jay.

45

Because you were so very kind
to those old dinosaurs,

you both deserve
these toys and treats.

Merry Christmas!

Santa Claus

Series editor: Lesley Sims

Reading consultant: Alison Kelly

First published in 2022 by Usborne Publishing Ltd., Usborne House,
83-85 Saffron Hill, London EC1N 8RT, England. usborne.com
Copyright © 2022 Usborne Publishing Ltd.

Look out for all the great stories in the Dinosaur Tales series!

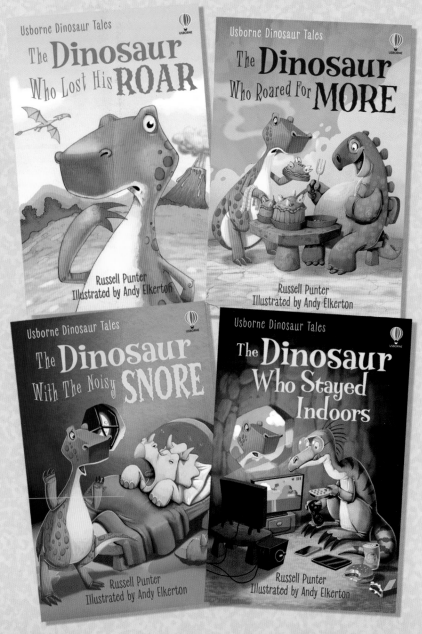